WHAT IT GROWING UP AS A GIRL ?

JOURNEY FROM THE SCORCHING SUN TO THE GLITTERING FABLES

NEHA GUPTA

Copyright © Neha Gupta
All Rights Reserved.

This book has been published with all efforts taken to make the material error-free after the consent of the author. However, the author and the publisher do not assume and hereby disclaim any liability to any party for any loss, damage, or disruption caused by errors or omissions, whether such errors or omissions result from negligence, accident, or any other cause.

While every effort has been made to avoid any mistake or omission, this publication is being sold on the condition and understanding that neither the author nor the publishers or printers would be liable in any manner to any person by reason of any mistake or omission in this publication or for any action taken or omitted to be taken or advice rendered or accepted on the basis of this work. For any defect in printing or binding the publishers will be liable only to replace the defective copy by another copy of this work then available.

Contents

Quote

*"What you think wouldn't get you what you want,
But What you do would definitely get you what you
deserve."*

Preface

The novel is written to accord with handicaps that the juveniles encounter in the community, owing to superstitious and orthodox norms. The fiction is revealing that, 'How A Girl Censure on every facet?' by the society. The tale also based on the character of a Boy who suffer heart attack when he breaks down to bring about what was expected from him by his dad.

The novella is based on the struggles of youths that put them into the flames of fire. Although, the purpose of this text is not to condemn anybody in the society or their pre-conceived notions but just to bring about that, "How are these communal standards putting effects on the hearts of our young generation in the nation and seizing their sigh?" The benchmarks are not awful at all if it makes the individual a decent human being or citizen of the country. But, be assured, the benchmarks don't capture the lives of noble human beings as well.

Acknowledgements

To become An Author, was just as a daydream for me. I can't imagine that I could ever take up writing as my career. It was just beyond my imagination that I would ever be apt, to turn my pieces, into the published novel. But All this become possible just because of the entire team of NotionPress who gave me platform to share my writings with the entire world. I just want to put my special thanks to the Founder, The Co-Founder, and The entire team of Instant Publication who support me to publish the Novel "What it feels like growing up as a girl?"

I wish to express my special thanks to my companions, who consistently crammed me with fresh intensity and spirit to pick up writing as a career. At the end, I wish to offer my special gratitude to all the readers who placed their valuable time and keen efforts to read out the text and make it more special.

About The Author

Neha Gupta is a fictional author, who always loves to write quotes, poetry and short tales on social issues. The motive behind her writings is to upliftment of the society. She has completed graduation and post-graduation in commerce field from the University of Delhi. She has 3+ years' experience of being a professional teacher. She has pen down in 30+ anthologies till now.

You can connect with her on her blog: authornehagupta.wordpress.com

About The Book

"What it feels like growing up as a girl?" is a fictional novel, written by Neha Gupta.

The novel makes up units that present the fable of an adolescent who was born and brought up in a culture where superstitious and orthodox norms are preeminent even if these preconceived norms smashed youngsters into chunks, and seize their breathe. Although, people used to assert that world is evolving. Yes, it is true, but, *"Can you just imagine the suicidal rates are still moving up at crest?"*, "What it holds when an adolescent is hurled into the conflagrations to explode?" The novel is written to inspire youth that you can accomplish everything if you hold belief in the spirit till the end, but you should have grit and eagerness to achieve it.

CHAPTER ONE

Snags In Youth's Life

Ananya, an adolescent who looks like an angel with glistening eyes and fascinating looks. She possesses a great mindset, but failed to get what she craves.

When she was 3 years old, she sent to school where she was inept to contend with other students as she feels burdensome to do rote learning and interpret the subjects, that were out of her interest and fetch top grades. Ananya's parents and the educators always oblige her to fetch excellent results in every subject. She was admonished and pummeled by her mom, if she failed to fetch excellent result in any subject.

She faced so many hardships in interpreting science book as she was impotent to apprehend the theory. She felt hesitate to ask anything to the educators in school as every other pupil in the class make fun of her, because she was a slow learner as compared to other pupils.

It was *8th September*, when she didn't understand the concept of *"Special Theory of Relativity"* in Science Course. She dared to ask her teacher Ms. Supriya, and said, *"Ma'am, Can you please clarify the concept of 'The special theory of*

Relativity' by Albert Einstein again...??"

Ma'am replied... "Why not, dear.....???"

"Sure, I will explain in the next class as it's time to take another class. Bye and have a nice day", said by Ms. Supriya.

On the next day, when she takes the class, she explains about *'The Special Theory of Relativity'* from the Scratch, as she vowed in the last class.

But, Ananya still failed to apprehend the same in the mind. It was terrible for her to interpret anything. Although, she tries to figure out the concept again and again. But, she gets panicked and didn't respond when the educator put up some questions in front of her, after delivering the lecture. She was scolded and bludgeoned by an educator in the front of the entire class, due to which she felt ashamed and abashed.

Miss. Supriya, the educator remarked to her that, "You are dumb and idiot to achieve anything. You would not grow and turn into a successful person ever, and you would just become a homemaker and mother of few kids."

Ananya felt shrieking and groaning, but couldn't speak out anything.

The entire class makes fun of her.

One of the girl laughing at her and said to her friend, I think, "Ananya is a loony and goofy girl."

Ananya felt embarrassed and mortified, but stayed silent and sit at backbench.

One boy, Aarav is staring and gazing at her, and felt that, "How adorable she looks when she weeps?" He wishes to move close to her and obliterate her woe and agony, but couldn't, as the entire class would chuckle if he goes on for the same.

On the same day, when she arrived at home. She expressed her affliction to her mother.

Her mom also criticized her and added, "You need to work hard and put extra efforts to get good grades, else you will consider as idiotic."

She had left with no choice, except just to do rote memorization of the black words that were printed in the textbook, and jot down the same in the examination hall.

Anyhow, she administered to qualify for the exams, but scourged by her mom at home when she looks at the grade card.

"Ooh! You got only passing score in science. It's a poor result. *What you used to do day and night that you are getting poor marks?*" She felt aching and distressing, that she goes to the bed without even having a bite of food and cried for the complete night.

Ananya thought for a while,

"Is it my life or someone else's life......???"

"Why can't I do what I wish to do......??"

"Why I need to study these textbooks and memorize these ridiculous concepts when I'm not at all excited about becoming scientist or engineer."

Not only this, but also "You would also be rebuked and reprimanded, if you would not get top grades in the class."

I wish if I could ever run out of such a dirty place where you don't have the right to elect anything conforming to your inclination and infatuation, but just facing physical and mental torment from parents and educationists for not picking up the greatest scores in the examination where values are just recognized as benchmarks for assessing intellectual level and success rate of pupils.

The annual function named 'Fiesta' has been organized at the end of the academic calendar. The name of participants has been picked for performance on fiesta, by the educator.

Ananya had took a decision to perform as she was very much passionate and keen to learn dance. She gave her name for the list promptly for being a participant on the Annual Function. She was thrilled and excited about pulling off her debut performance. She picked out the song, which was enticing as well as trending.

One of her fella said, *"you should pitch in on a medley of songs as it was very dernier cri nowadays."*

Ananya reached at home and informed about the annual function to her mom, *Divya*.

Divya was feeling extremely happy, and appreciate her by saying, "Great! I am delighted for my son to take such opportunities in life."

Ananya wants to dance on the floor as it was the first time that she was praised by her mother.

But she was little confused about that, *"Why Divya called her a son...??"*

So, Ananya pointed out to her mother and asked "Why did you call me son? I'm your daughter and not a son."

Ooh Beta! But, " 'you are like my son.' Now, start practicing for your dance performance on the Annual Day," Divya replied.

Sure, I'm going, but I want to ask, Was it bad to call a girl, *'A Girl'*?

I think 'No'.

So, just call me 'a Girl, *not a boy*' and I feel it's not right, if I call your son, 'a girl, *not a boy*.'

*****

4

CHAPTER TWO

CHIT CHAT WITH FELLA...!!

She comes into the room and tries to find out a splendid song to play on the stage. She picked up a song that was gravitating and classic.

She felt that, *"I would absolutely gonna sway on the stage if I'll perform on this song."*

One of her fella, Swati also arrived at home and said, 'Hey Ananya, have you selected the song...???'

Let me know about the song that you have chosen. Swati asked.

"Hi Swati, Why not...?? But first, squat on the chair and let's have some snacks and juices as it was the first time you turned at my home."Ananya replied.

"Don't do these rites, Ananya. I'm not a guest here, I deem. I'm your close buddy." Swati said.

"Actually, I have placed an order for Chèze burst pizza, Hakka noodles and Cold drinks for evening snacks. 'Don't you crave to have a piquant slice of pizza, Swati?' " Ananya told.

Wow...! Chèze Burst Pizza and noodles with cold drink, are so tempting and savoury.

OK ok! I would obviously love to have zesty wedges of pizza, 'How much time would it take to turn up here?' Swati said.

Just wait for 10 minutes. Let's have a chit chat till then. Ananya said.

By the Way! Did you notice...?? Aarav was gawking at you when you felt weepy in the class. He was also smiling by gazing at you. I can discern that he falls in love with you.

'Don't you feel the same?' Swati asked.

Ooh! But, I do not know about the same, Swati. And I prefer to fixate on my career right now.

So, 'just make him understand he stays away from me if he has the feelings for me.' I never want to pamper in all this, as I don't want to break trust of my kinsfolk.

My brother would have made me sit at home, if he ever come to know that I have a boyfriend. Ananya told.

Meanwhile, the doorbell rang.

Swati said, "I think, the delivery boy has arrived."

Yeah! Let me get it fast. Ananya replied.

Ananya opens the gate and picks up the pizza, noodles and cold drink from the delivery boy.

When Ananya opens the pizza box. Swati said, *"Aha! Yummy pizza and noodle. I can't wait anymore to devour my favourite Chèze burst pizza with cold drink."*

"Haha! So, why do you have to wait? Let's put red chilli flakes and oregano seasoning over it and then take yummy and creamy Chèze pizza in the mouth."Ananya replied.

While enjoying pizza, Ananya could have been recalled that, 'Swati wants to know about the song that she singled out for the dance performance.'

Ananya told to Swati, "Hey! I want to tell you that I am going to perform on 'Coca Cola' song."

Waooo..! Then, you would surely go to rock on the stage. And Aarav would also feel intimacy and affection towards you. HaHaHa...! Swati said.

Ooh! Just shut your mouth and stop teasing me. I truly don't wish to have any relationship with him, Ananya replied.

When Ananya start practicing rehearsal of tango, Aarav usually stares at her and notices her gestures. 'His eyes sparkle and face grinned whenever he gazes at her!'

*****

CHAPTER THREE

COLLIDE WITH KINSFOLK...!!!

After a few days, Ananya informed about the annual function to her dad, Saransh, and seek for the cash to purchase a costume and other adornments that required for her show.

Saransh reacted astonishingly, "Ooh Really...!!, Are you sure? I wish, you would have been able to perform on the stage confidently and don't seem perturbed at the last juncture."

Why would I get panicked, dad...? I could manage everything.Ananya replied.

Divya also interrupt and asked, "Why would she get panicked...?" I have faith in her. Rest if she will, let her be. Else, "How would she grow up and learn to perform on the stage?" It was the exact place where she could remove her hesitation as she was performing in school, not on the platform of "Dance India Dance."

Yeah! "That's also made up a point, let her be." said by Saransh. And, we should appreciate her for such a step, "as every step in the life prepares us to grow and take further challenges."

"No one can grow until he takes risk in life."

Now, "Can I have money in my pocket so that I can walk out for shopping with my friends?" Ananya asked.

Sure, you can grab one thousand rupees from my bag and get your stuff. Saransh replied.

What have you said, dad....? merely Rs. 1000? Are you making fun of me? What would I get with this amount? I could not purchase even a dress for 1000 rupees.

"How much you require, then?" Dad asked to Ananya.

I need approx Rs. 5k dad. Ananya replied.

What...? Are you crazy, Ananya? You need 5k for the performance for one day. I can't give you Rs. 5k. I think you shouldn't go ahead. Saransh told.

No, I couldn't move back now. Please give 5k dad. Ananya requested.

I can't manage Ananya, you should either quit from the show or arrange the money by yourself. Saransh replied.

Ananya seemed to be dismayed and worried. She gets muddled that, "Whether she should move forward or pull out her name...??"

Ananya makes a call to Swati and thrash out everything with her. Swati replied, "Why don't you pick up everything on rent?, It wouldn't cost much."

Ananya also gets agree on the point and arranged everything on rent for two days.

On the day of "Fiesta", she was looking glamorous in the costume.Aarav reacted, "Hey! Is she Ananya...??" and said, "I'm not able to recognize her as she was looking so pretty."

He was chuckling and gazing at her.

When Ananya moved to the stage, she gets panicked, but closed her eyes for a second and calmed herself, after which she performed very well that she set the stage on fire.

The audience had watched her performance with rapt attention, appreciate her hard work. The "fiesta" function ended with the hand out of rewards and certificates.

The days passed, and she passed 10th class, which was the ecstatic time for her as she passed over all the breakthroughs in the school and hardly 2 years left, to exit the haunting place. But, "what's the question now that, Which stream should she embrace?"

She was not intended to take up science ever as it was extremely loathe subject for her. She could have foreseen herself quashed in future by holding up science subject as it was distressing for her to fathom the concept.

She preferred commerce, but her parents compel her to prefer for science stream as it had a great scope for the future. But, she turned down the suggestion and replied, "Sorry dad, I could not take up science stream as it puts me in a terrible situation when I comprehend the subject. I went through psychological pressure when I pore over the science subject. It was rote learning subject for me which I couldn't endure. And don't push me to take up science, else you would find me suffering delirious situation one day. I want to hold that subject with which I could enjoy my life as well. I don't want to be a bookworm girl. I prefer to do something that was distinctive and groundbreaking. I would opt for a professional course after schooling."

"Well, it was also a great idea, but you should consider twice as it was the stream that was taken up by intellectual and superior mindsets. And you could go for prestigious and technical profession like Doctor, engineer and architect etc." Dad replied.

But, *what if I could not linger with the subject? And also put myself into inferno one day. What you feel if I couldn't sigh effortlessly after obtaining lavish Car and Air condition rooms that could have happened with me if I study science. None of the subject and the Career are suitable for you until you revel in it and lead your life.* Ananya said.

*****

CHAPTER FOUR

STEPPING STONES DURING COLLEGE LIFE

Ananya walked out of the school, that was just a fuss for her. She perceived it as a hustle because it was the place of rules and regulations that was just a chip on her shoulder.

On the first day, Ananya gets baffled with, "What should she wear?" On the one hand, she has been in contemplation that she might put on one piece as it was the first day.

What if she would have been wearing shalwar suit? Everybody will make fun of her and remark to her as "Benjy or Aunty". So, she had decided to wear one piece as it makes her sound extremely beautiful, but when she arrived at the college, the boys molest her by calling "Ohhh! Too sexy she is ....."

And the lad turned on bike gawking at her and called her, "you are splendid, babe." Would you like to date me.....??? And pass flying kiss to her.......!!

Ananya had felt peeved and vexed. But, she had neglected and get in the class for taking lecture.

Meanwhile, she had interacted with classmates who were immensely impeccable and didn't benchmark character of any person with "what they wore..!!". She figured out that "They are perfect guys for turning into my buddies."

On the next day, when she would have been getting ready for the college, she considered again that "What should she put on?" She had got so many remarks from lads on the first day of the college, owing to which she is in anguish.

After a while, she put on a shalwar suit along with matching bangles. And, she arrived at the college where she had shrewd that some guys were peering at her.

Although, no judgments had been passed, but yes! They had put an eyeball on her due to which she finds herself in a bizarre situation.

Before Ananya enters the class, she deciphers a notice that was put up on the bulletin board, on which it was written that "Dance club would have been starting on 21st July. If anybody prefers to be part of it, he/she can visit administration department of Dance Club, for further details and process."

Ananya was truly interested in prom. So, she had joined a dance club. She had gone to the Administration department and enroll herself. One of her chum, named Sanya Ahuja, also joined the club.

When she moves out of the college, she had been waiting for the bus at a nearby bus station. Meanwhile, a guy on the bike arrived at the moment and asked to her, "Can I drop you at your home?"

Ananya felt aghast and offended for a while. She replied, "No, I will go by bus." After a bit, the bus turned up, and she enters inside the bus and left the place. She reached at home and took the food.

On finding her daughter disturbed because of some reason. The mother asked. 'What happen to you?', 'Are you ok?'

Ananya didn't respond and move into her bedroom. She hadn't slept for the complete night as she felt worried and restless. At 2a.m., she received a message from an anonymous number. Her phone popped up with the message, "Hi, how are you?" Suddenly, her eyes opened and she felt startled to receive the text in her inbox at this moment. She moved out of the room instantly and gets confused as *she gets perplexed*... 'who he is...?', 'Is this number belongs to her fellow friends?', 'Why is he texting me at this point of time?'

She texted to her buddy, "Hi Manvi, sorry to disturb you at this moment, but I'm in trouble. I just received a text message from an anonymous but I can't recognize the number. Do you know the name of the person to whom this number belongs to?"

The eyes of Manvi open abruptly, and she checked out the message.

Manvi replied, "The number is not saved in my contact list. May be, Someone had sent the text by mistake."

You can go to have placid sleep now. It's too late to have a chat, and in case,"if, my parents get up, they would think that I'm bustled in chatting with my beau."

Hahaha.....!!! Ananya giggled.

Ok sweetheart, you can go for sleep. Bye, goodnight and take care. Ananya replied.

"Ok baby, you too." Manvi replied.

Ananya forgets about the text message for a while after having a gossip with Manvi. She fled back to the bed and trying to sleep.

After a while, she could have been recalled whatever happen last day with her on the bus station and, impugned, "May be, the number belongs to that stranger boy."

On the next day, she ate Chèze sandwich along with choco brownie shake for breakfast. At 6:40 a.m., she picks up a bag and moves out for the college.

She reached college at around 9a.m. After reaching at college, she was meshing with her friends and also trying to dig up, "Who has texted her last night ?"After sometime, she saw the same boy who was staring at her, but she scorned and move ahead.

As she had to attend Math's Lecture, so she had had to stay in the college till 5p.m. But, when she moves out of the class after taking lecture, the anonymous person block her way to step forward and asked, "Did you get my message that I have dropped last night?"

Ananya turns into a quarrelsome girl, and asked him... "Who you are?", "How did you get my contact?", "How dare you to text me late at night?"

Oh! Ma'am, hold for a bit and give me a few minutes to say something. "I don't have any wrong intentions. I just like you as a friend, and I was just teasing you, but sorry if I put you in trouble, *"Can't we become good friends?"*

Ooh! Ok fine, no issues, "Sure, we can turn into good buddies. But, May I know your name...?? and Are you pursuing the same course that is of me...??" Ananya asked.

"Ooh! you don't know my name.",the Boy said in a horrific tone.

By the way..! My name is Ishaan, "Would you like to have lunch with me?"

"No, not for today. I have to take the lecture."

"Ooh lecture! that's too necessary. Ok, no issue, Bye and take care. Nice girl you are..!!!," said Ishaan.

"Thanks Ishaan, nice to meet you." Ananya replied.

*****

CHAPTER FIVE

TURNING OF CAMARADERIE INTO RELATIONSHIP

Ishaan and Ananya chat with each other at night frequently. But, sometimes, they get indulged in arguing on silly issues but forgive each other after sometime.

The time has been passed, and their bonding gets deeper within sometime. Ishaan felt some special feelings towards Ananya. But, he prefers not to express it as he thought "their bonds might have been broken by revealing his sentiments to Ananya." So, he holds his affection to himself, but he loves Ananya so much that he always used to treat her childishly.

Sometimes, *"he kids her by calling a baby."*

Or... *"Hayy! Meri Jaan, you are too gorgeous and pretty."*

Or...., *"Abee moti! How much you used to eat? You have been gaining weight too much."*

He consistently checks her online status in the night until she bedded down. If any other boy talks to her, he becomes jealous and intrusive. He used to thrust punch covertly on the face of a boy who came close to her or propose her. But, he constantly goes on all such acts in a way that Ananya couldn't even doubt...

When Ananya performs a tango on the stage in a dancing competition. *Ishaan looks at her and holds that "she is the best dancer in the world."*

But, *he kids her by asserting, "I hope the stage would not be broken by you one day, moti."*

Haha! Are you cracking joke? Ananya said.

"No, I'm saying earnestly, you truly dance pretty well." Ishaan told.

"Can we visit chit-chat café today? You have no lecture today." Ishaan asked.

Ananya reacted, "No, I can't go out with you, Ishaan."

But, "Why are you turning down my offer to walk out with me? Don't you trust me or what?" Ishaan asked.

No yr, nothing like that. Actually, "my dad doesn't allow me to move out with boys. And my brother is going to kill me if he would look at that I am driving out and devouring with boys." Ananya told.

Ishaan enquired, "Why would he kill you?", "Is he psychotic?"

No, that's not the reason. I am a girl, and I couldn't move out with lads because of security issues. Ananya replied.

Oh, ok! Let's book a car, so that no one can look at us when we walk out. Ishaan replied.

Ananya retorted, "No, *this is unethical, dude.*" conforming to my standards.

Meanwhile, the classmate of Ananya, called Vedika, enters the class.

Vedika spoke "hi guys, how are you?" to both Ananya and Ishaan.

"We are fine. How are you dude?" said Ishaan.

Vedika told "good sweetheart."

Ishaan said, "I am going out Vedika. Would you like to join me?"

"Sure, why not?" Vedika replied.

Great! Ishaan held her hand and step out with Vedika from the college.

Ananya would have been observing everything, but didn't add a word. She sensed something in her heart at the moment, but what...?

Ananya couldn't recognize. When she had reached at her home and asked her Mom, "What have you cooked, Mom?"

"Rajma Rice and chapatti.", the mom responded.

Ananya gets into the room to cool off. Meanwhile, the mom serves the appetizing food on the table.

While having meal, Ananya was cussing Ishaan,"Why did he went out with Vedika?", "Why did he hold her hand?" She had finished her food hastily, and get onto the bed to have sleep. But, on seeing that, Ishaan was active on WhatsApp right now. she sent a text to the Ishaan, "Hey, have you taken the food?"

But Ishaan ignored the message of Ananya.

Ananya felt so painful, but opt to keep her mouth shut. She perceived that, "Ishaan might have been talking to Vedika."

*****

CHAPTER SIX

MESSED UP BETWEEN CAREER OPTIONS

The Ananya was pondering one day in the dawn, "What I have to do after graduation?" My dad would prefer for me to study further and opt for masters. But, I don't want to engross in studies. I wish to own my business so that I could revel in my life, and I could have infinite income. I know,"*it would take a lot of hard work. But one day, I could have my own splendid car, house and good-looking husband, who can fulfil all needs of my heart.*" But, what about my dad.....? Would he permit me to do business?

Most probably 'No' as it was also the place where girls are called stupid, even if she reflects an idea about the business. Lets see, "what will happen later?" For now, I have to focus on exams else I will be castigated again to get low marks.

When Ishaan reached at the college, she asked Ishaan, "what would you do after graduation?"

I haven't decided yet but maybe I would like to prepare for UPSC exams. My dad always dreamt of viewing me as an IAS officer. I could do everything to make him feel honored. Ishaan replied.

Wow! You are so sweet, Ishaan, who thinks so much about parents. I wish, "you achieve all what you want." Well, "what would you do baby after graduation?" Ishaan asked to Ananya.

Ananya, in belligerent mood, replied, *"Baby.... ??, Why have you called me baby? I* am not your baby and all. Got it...?" Chill! Just teasing,"Why do you become contentious rapidly?" "Who would love you if you react in such a manner?" Grow up girl and be open-minded, Ishaan retorted.

Ooh! Don't suggest to me your weird opinions. I don't need your advice. "By the way, I will set up my business afterwards," replied Ananya.

Hahaha, "What......?", "What have you said...?", "Are you out of your senses....?" Ishaan asked.

'Do you know, you are a girl ?' Business requires a lot of resources and investment. "Who would invest in your business?" Ishaan added.

But why? Because I'm a lady...? Is gender spelled out "what could I do or what not?", I couldn't discover any logic behind it. Ananya said.

No Ananya...that's not my point ...but, *Do you think that you can manage business efficiently?,* Who will invest in your venture?, How would you carry out financial and non-financial resources? Ishaan asked.

"Why couldn't I Ishaan?" I'm Damm sure that I could turn into a lucrative entrepreneur. Yeah! it's true I haven't worked out on anything till now but I will. Ananya responded.

Vedika interrupt and inquired, "What you guys are talking about?"

Ananya was thinking about setting up her own business. So, I was just recommending that business can't be handled by girls. It calls for a lot of hard work and fortitude. And girls are unfit for picking up such an encumbrance on her head. Apart from that, she also needs to look at her family due to which she hardly gets anytime for business. Ishaan replied.

Hahaha...What a ludicrous guy you are, Ishaan? Vedika replied.

I know we are she's. It doesn't mean that we can't handle business or anything else. We could run business better than you boys. You enjoy your government job in which barely 10% of students get shortlisted out of overall appeared applicants. And let Ananya look at what she prefers to do. You are not here to determine, "What a girl can do or what not?" If you can't encourage her, then at least don't impede her as well. Vedika added.

Ananya seemed elated when Vedika took her favour. She felt encouraging and appreciating and added, "Eventually, I got someone here to support me."

Vedika asked to Ishaan..., "What will you do if you wouldn't get a government job?"

Why don't I get? I will do hard work day and night with full dedication, and get my name on the list of selected candidates. Ishaan replied.

Still, there are lakhs of people who apply for UPSC exams every year and, they failed to qualify for the exam. "What if you also get fail and not able to qualify?" Vedika rebutted.

Don't discourage me. I perceive I could make it, if not in the 1st attempt, surely, be in 4th or 5th attempt. Ishaan replied.

I admire your spirit, Ishaan. I hope you could make it. Vedika said.

Meanwhile, the professor of accounts begins the class and spoke, "Hello! Good morning students, How are you students?"

Well, good sir, the students responded.

So, today, we would study about balance sheet.

A girl Priyanshi, squat beside Ishaan, said, "oh! Too tedious yr."

Ananya further added, "yeah! Correct. It's too monotonous and laborious as well. My mind gets mesh up with infinite formulas in the exam."

"Shut your mouth and focus on studies for now." Ishaan interrupts.

"How much studious you are?" Priyanshi asked.

Shut up! I prefer to study so that I could be an IAS officer and make my parents honored. You ladies would not understand, as you don't have obligations to fulfil the needs of your clan. You would have to get married and look out for infants. But, "what about me?" No girl would wed me until I got a government job. Now, focus on lecture. We would continue our discussion afterwards. Ishaan replied in aggressive mood.

Ok sure, Priyanshi replied.

The educator has been delivering a lecture on Balance Sheet. He was expounding about accounting standards that every student should hold in mind while preparing the balance sheet.

He observed some students were busy in chattering on WhatsApp. The lecturer gets little aggressive over such behavior on which he yelled and ordered students to switch off their phone and put it in a pocket. He had further expressed hatred speeches for next 20 minutes over such acts. And warn that, if I spotted you are using phone during the lecture again, you would be marked with zero in your internals.

Priyanshi muttered, "the educators couldn't control their intimidate behaviour ever."

Some students replied, "We apologize sir, it would never happen again."

Good! "I would have been expecting the same." the professor responded.

The lecture gets over, and they fled towards the cafeteria for lunch.

So, "what are you saying, Priyanshi and Ananya, at the time of the lecture?" Now, we have enough of time to talk about that. Let's confer it now. Ishaan said.

"Why don't you set up your own business?" Ananya asked.

"It requires finance, and it further takes much time to establish. I could not think even that I could run a business successfully." Ishaan responded.

Can I order noodles and samosa for you guys? Vedika interrupts.

Wow! Cool Vedika, Give Order of two samosas for me. Ananya replied.

Haha! You should consume limited junk food moti as you have been picking up weight. Ishaan again starts pestering her. Ishaan grinned.

Ooh! just shut your mouth. You would not marry me, so you might avoid fretting about me, and you must look for a slim young woman to be your spouse. I've no issue if have been picking up weight. *"If anybody prefers to accept me, he should accept in the way what I am not, what he wants."* Ananya reverts.

Ok. sorry dear. I would not go on this further. Let's get back to our discussion. Ishaan said.

Yeah! I want to mention that, 'if your business gets succeed, your income might be in crores one day. You could have everything that you call for. I don't think that government jobs could provide that much pay. Ananya said.

But it adds to goodwill in the community, and I wish to contribute to my nation. I could take steps to wipe out starvation, crime on young woman, child labour issues, and other social issues. Ishaan said.

Oh well! But what would you do with that.....???? What about your wealth......????

Goodwill don't bring up wealth. They would just add to your social prestige that you can fetch too when you establish your own business, and fill your pocket with crores like Mukesh Ambani, etc.

Why are you guys debating over one point since the morning? Vedika interrupt.

Do you have any issue? We are deliberating to have a beneficial career ahead. If you have any issue, you can sit at some alternative place. Ishaan reacted.

"I apologize Ananya, break off the conversation. You guys carry on." Vedika added to Ananya.

It's ok. I have been knackered too over this topic now. I realize everyone has their own point of view. I appreciate your opinions, Ishaan, as it took fortitude to hold the vision of becoming IAS officer and gear up for UPSC exams. Ananya said.

*****

CHAPTER SEVEN

PLANNING OF EXCURSION TO GOA

Well! I have been planning for a trip to Goa in the upcoming month.

Would you guys like to join me? Vedika spoke.

"Yeah! I am.", Ishaan told.

Have you planned anything like timing, days, charges, transport, etc. till now? Many other comrades, that are, Alankrita, Vishal, Priyanshi, Kritika and 20 others felt psyched for the excursion to Goa. Ishaan asked.

No, I haven't worked out on anything till now. Initially, I would rather prefer to have an estimated idea about the total students who are interested, and I want to concoct the list of those students, and also, I would collect half of the amount as an advance to book the seat, so that we could go ahead. Further, we also need to share responsibility among us, so that all the arrangements could be pulled together by everyone to carry out the plan successfully and effectively. Vedika responded.

The onus to collect the money could be handled by Seema Jain. Then, the arrangement of the transport could be looked up by Rahul, and the hotels could be managed by Priyanshi.

In addition, "We would also hire one tourist guide person so that it would be easier for us to have fun at various captivating places and monuments of Goa." Vedika said.

Sure, I would handle the responsibility of looking out for the best tourist guide. Ishaan told.

Ok guys! that's enough. But, be sure that no one is going to back out in the end. Vedika said.

No No! not at all. We are indeed intrigued more than you for our first trip to Goa. Simran reacted.

Ok guys! Now, what you have to do next, "Get and deposit two thousand as security in advance to book your seat." Ananya said.

Ok we will....!! everyone responded, and step out of the college after shaking hands with each other as usual.

On the next day. "I hope you all guys have brought two thousand rupees to deposit as advance." Ishaan asked.

Yes Ishaan! Priyanshi and other peer members responded.

Why are you mum, Ananya? Is there any issue? Your eyes are also looking puffy. Haven't you slept properly in the night? Vedika sought.

No! Nothing dear. I'm completely fine and ok. There is nothing to worry about. Ananya replied.

Oh Really! Do you think I'm a naïve in recognizing your facial expression? You are free to talk to me about any kind of issue. Does anything wrong with your family? Vedika pointed out.

Ananya turned into a lachrymose woman and said, "Actually, my parents do not permit me to step out of the town for excursion."

But why yr...? What's the issue with your parents? Vedika asked.

It's your life and you should decide, "If you want to head out or not, and where?" You have been a grown-up lady and you must be told this to your parents. Ishaan suggested.

I'm just fed up with my parents and their grotesque norms. They don't permit me for anything. You shouldn't do this or you should do like this, you shouldn't go out or you should go out with us only. I couldn't argue with them, even else they would rebuke me and say, "Oh! you have grown up so much that you are arguing with us. We are your parents and you should obey our views and thoughts. We already have enough of experiences of everything but you have just grown up, so carry on what we are recommending to you. We are your parents, not your enemies. Why do we think bad about you? It's safe if you stay at home."

According to them, it was just a waste of hard-earned money out of their pocket to go for the excursion. They want me to focus on my studies or, if not, then look for household work. Ananya told.

But, we wouldn't enjoy without you in Goa, babe. "Can we talk to your parents....?"

Or,"Can we contribute from our side if you want to go....?"

You don't need to return any money back. We want you to stay happy always. Vedika said.

No, they wouldn't permit me to go on a trip even if you guys try too, to coax my parents or arrange everything at free of cost. They are too much stringent and stereotype people.

"I also curse myself to be the daughter of such kind of stubborn parents. But, I couldn't even tell this to anybody else, else I would be a shameless daughter in their eyes because you can't curse your parents if you born as a citizen of such patriarchal society."

They would prefer to cook food, wash clothes and clean utensils for me at home if I prefer not to study, but not to go anywhere.

Or, if I would argue with them, they would start looking for a groom for me. It was hard to tolerate such nuisance of my family. Ananya said.

Haha...I couldn't stop myself from chuckling. I think you should focus on your study. I couldn't say anything more.

I'm literally shocked by the demeanor of your parents. But stop weeping now. I hope everything would get fine when you achieve something great in your life. Vedika said.

You would definitely be granted for everything that you want, when you get success. And after all, you want to opt for business, so you would be a businesswoman later. You can go anywhere, wherever you want, and can take your decisions." What if you cannot go this time? We would definitely go together when you will establish your own business." So just be chill, sweetheart. Ishaan replied.

Ananya cuddled Ishaan tightly and said, Thanks, Ishaan, for your kind and sweet words.

Everyone gets silenced for a few minutes, and Ishaan was like, "Oh my God! Ananya embraced me..." It was a best moment for me ever. For a while, he thought to kiss her, but anyhow, control himself.

After a few minutes of silence. Rahul interrupt and asked, "I think a train would be a better option as it was the cheapest mode of transport."

Ishaan said...yeah ok.

But Vedika refused and said "No yr, I think we should depart by car as it was full Air conditioned."

Hahaha... Ishaan laughed and said, "Do you know how much it will cost to go by bus........???"

Rahul said to Ishaan, "so, it's not a big deal for Vedika."

Vedika replied... What do you mean, Rahul?

Nothing. I was just saying that you can reach Goa by car. Others would go by train as we can't afford to go by car. And it will suit your standard too...!!Rahul replied.

Haww! Vedika staring at him annoyingly.

I am just kidding Vedika...Don't stare at me so dangerously...!! I am feeling so scary. Rahul replied.

"Would you like to have a punch from my hand, here or somewhere else, Rahul...?" I would not spare you now. Vedika rebutted.

Och! I'm quivering.... Haha... Rahul snickered.

Meanwhile, the bell buzzed for the next lecture.

Ok guys..., let's get ready to take the lecture. We would proceed further after taking the irksome lecture. Rahul said.

Hey, 'How was it if we bunk the lecture for today?' We have bunked no lecture till now, and it was not at all good if college students haven't bunked the class ever. Vedika asked.

No, we shouldn't bunk the class. These lectures would benefit us throughout the life, and we could have an excellent result at the end of the course. Ishaan recommended.

You are immensely tedious boy, Ishaan. Don't be so serious. We should also relish our life along with studies."*Studies are the part of life, not the entire way to live life.*" Vedika countered.

By the way, what about others? Are you also interested in taking lecture? Vedika added.

Ananya also turned down, as her mood is already spoiled because of his parents, and other classmates also refused to bunk the class.

"Are you really so interested in your studies?" Vedika responded.

Yes! You should too, take your studies seriously. We could have merriment in free classes, no need to bunk lecture for that. Studies are very relevant for future, so grab it vigorously. Ishaan responded.

Ok Ishaan. I'm taking the lecture now. Would you avoid delivering your lecture to me? Vedika reacted.

The lecture concluded and everybody carry on with discussion.

"I figure out 'bloom suites' would be the finest hotel to stay in Goa. It was one of the best hotels." Rahul told.

Yes, it was one of the fantastic hotels in Goa. You can book this hotel. Ishaan and Vedika also added.

And what about food, as we are going out for 4 days and 3 nights? Rahul asked.

We would get food in the hotel. But if you want to carry something with you to eat during the travel or some other reason, you can get it from your side. Priyanshi responded.

Ishaan noted that, "Ananya was having worst feeling when everyone is planning for a trip to Goa." Ishaan was feeling lousy for her, but he can't do anything as it was her parents who rebuffed her to move out of the town.

But, he counselled her and said, "Don't worry dear, there would definitely a day when you travel the entire world with your hard-earned money, and you don't need to seek anyone's permission."

31

Ananya was feeling happy that someone is there, who understands her from heart and soul.

"Which are the famous places there to travel where we would go?" Seema asked.

Oh! Goa has so many places to have fun like Palolem Beach (famous beach of Goa), basilica de Bom Jesus (religious site), Dudhsagar falls (Aquatic Adventure), Braganza house (Mahadeva temple), Sunset at Utorda beach. Vedika said.

"It has 'Club Titos' too, to have fun in the night. We could have a party, dance, singing, food, drinks and mingle with friends. You would have a special feeling that you haven't felt ever before." Priyanshi said.

Anjuna beach is also one of the best beaches in Goa. Anjuna is the epitome of euphoria. When the soothing music reaches you and the waves touch down on your feet; it is blissful! Alankriti said.

Shiva Valley which is also one of the famous cafes for every kind of taste and ravishing moment. It's wonderful for all of us where we could hear the crashing waves, enjoy a lovely crowd and the vibrant bright colours that dangle from ceilings, and make the aura trippy. Seema said.

Ok buddies! So, we would visit as many places as we can. Priyanshi said.

Yeah! Priyanshi. I'm avidly waiting for that day when we would depart for Goa with gusto, as it was my first trip. I would carry one-piece dresses for waterfronts and night clubs so that I would look captivating and ravishing. Vedika spoke.

'Oh! You would look so hot and sexy then.' Rahul grinned.

"Keep your tongue within a limit. It's not good if I turn into an angry bird and remark you with cuss words." Vedika said.

It's just a fun. It's ok to have that much fun with friends. You should not mind, and even you should enjoy it. Ishaan grinned.

Ooh Really! Can't I perceive, "Is it a fun or what?" Keep your fun with yourself, else it would turn into an erotic relationship one day, and still you would say that "it's just a fun."

Ok! don't give a lecture yr and chill out. Priyanshi mentioned.

*****

CHAPTER EIGHT

LIFE CHANGING FRACAS

Ok fine! I'm walking out to chow down the slices of pizza in dominos nearby. Vedika said.

"Why are you going out to have pizza? Is it your birthday today, Vedika?" Ananya reacted.

No Ananya! My birthday falls on 23rd Feb, but, Why are you wondering about it? Vedika replied.

Ok! Ok! I guessed you are giving a birthday party. Hehe. Ananya said.

Can't we do party without having a birthday or something special? 'I think we can go to have a party or anything else on normal days as well, having no special occasion. Isn't it?' Vedika reacted.

Yes, we can do party and enjoy our life anytime. Ananya said.

By the way! I omit to inform you that, "I heard Dominos are offering 1pkt of pasta and 1 small coke along with pizza for a week." Vedika told.

Oh! It was so pampering offer. Let's move out all together to have savory and luscious veg overloaded pizza along with the tangy snacks. Priyanshi told.

When they are on the way to Dominos. Few lads are passing nearby. One boy continuously gawking at the girls and passed a comment,'Wow! you are too hot babes yr......!!!'

Yeah! they are extremely seductive and slinky. They are perfect girls to have sex. Let's ask them for a date. Another person expressed.

Rahul and Ishaan noticed everything and tuned into aggressive people, and start wrangling with the street romeos."Why don't you guys keep yourself away? It would not be good for you if we punch you badly. So, keep yourself away." One of the freaking person said.

Oh! would you punch us.......??????

Ok, come on. Rahul said.

All the boys rolled their sleeves up and start fighting with each other.

One boy put a comment. "Are you going to marry with these girls? If not, why are you grudging if we would bed down with them just for a night? We wouldn't hurt them, we would just express our warmth feelings towards them."

"We don't need to explain to you what we are or what not." Ishaan and Rahul throw a big punch to their faces after that.

Rahul and Ishaan get scratched on body parts, and girls are feeling anxious when they are viewing all this nuisance with their open eyes.

The girls interrupt in-between and try to protect Rahul and Ishaan.

Meanwhile, A boy pressed Vedika's breast and touch hips to have sensational feelings at the same time. But, Vedika felt it and slapped a boy tightly.

'How dare you are to slap me? You are a girl and be within your limits.' The boy reacted.

"And how dare you to touch me? You aren't allowed to do anything what you want, if you are a boy." Vedika said.

"You are so hot and sexy, babe!" I can't hold myself to have sex with you. Would you like to sleep with me? I would give you 10 lakh sweetheart, Don't defy my offer...!!!

Ishaan and Rahul quarreled again with those boys.

Ishaan and Rahul hold the hand of that boy, and asked Vedika, "To take out your shoes and hit on his face."

But, the Another boy took out the acid and throw on Vedika's face from the back.

Everyone got stunned, and the boys run away from the place. Rahul had called the ambulance and the police.

The police reached the site within ten to fifteen minutes. The police officers verified each and everything on the site. They had also inquired about the incident from beginning.

After a few minutes, the ambulance also reached at the site within 20 minutes, and took her to the hospital.

The parents of Vedika arrived at the hospital and bothered a lot. They asked to Ishaan and Rahul, "how's my daughter now?"

The face of Vedika has been combusted awfully, and some droplets of acid falls on her hands as well. Right now, she is in operation theatre. I hope everything would get fine promptly. Ishaan replied.

The parents of Vedika waited for two hours outside the operation theatre and their heart was pumping hard.

Finally, after two and the half hours, the surgeons came out and informed to her parents that we should have to go for surgery on the face of Vedika else stains of acid attack would remain long lasting.

Rahul said, "ok, you can go ahead for surgery, and save her life."

We would proceed further, but it would put a burden of around 20 lakhs on your head. Dr Sachin responded.

Aww.....!!! 20 lakhs. It was too much. "How would we manage 20 lakhs?" the parents expressed in a terrible sound.

"It's not my issue. You could take the time of two days to deposit the money, if not, you could take your girl at home with scars." Dr Sachin replied.

*****

CHAPTER NINE

THE UPSHOT OF CONTRETEMPS

Ananya, who stands aside, said, "Let do one thing, we could contribute for her. We all will pitch in together what all we have, for Vedika, and definitely save her precious life."

Not merely this, we could further collect donations from the students and the staff members of our college. Rahul suggested.

Yeah! It was obviously an excellent idea. Priyanshi said.

So, guys, what we are waiting for? Let's walk out and collect money from the home and the other sources. Then, we all would gather in the college to collect charities. Ishaan said.

Everyone fled towards home to collect money and later reached at the college at around 5 p.m.

Ishaan said, "hey! I have brought eighty thousand rupees. How much you guys got? Let's calculate and put all the money together in a bag."

Overall, we have around five lakh rupees. Let's call for a contribution from the members of the college. Rahul said.

Yeah! ok. But what would we convey to them? How does all this take place abruptly? Priyanshi asked.

We need to think about it, Priyanshi. Ananya replied.

But why can't we tell that, "a boy throws acid on her face due to which she has been admitted in hospital, and she needs support. After all, we have tried hard to save her life, and the incident crops up because of those culprits. We have done no atrocity." Rahul sought.

Yeah! You, all are right, Rahul..

But, try to understand that she is a young woman. 'If we say that someone throws acid on her face, no one would like to see her, met her and talk to her. Her relationships got affected as well.' Ananya told.

So, what if she is a girl.....? She did nothing wrong. Rahul said.

But who will take notice of her?

Everybody would say that the girls should have required to maintain their limits. They shouldn't walk out with male members, they shouldn't quarrel with males, they should stay silent and all that. 'And the girls would also feel hesitant to step outside of the college.' Priyanshi spoke.

Maybe. it's your point of view Priyanshi, but I do not afraid to say truth. After all, all should know about the crimes that were cropping up around us in our community. I will go ahead with realism, and I truly don't care "what others think?"

People realize the agony of others when they suffer the same plight, and I want to ask, " Would you also look at the same stuff when it crops up on you or your sibling?", "Would you disguise your face because of societal pressure?" Rahul said.

"No, not at all", Priyanshi spoke.

Then, "why have you been holding different opinions for Vedika?" Rahul asked.

Yes, you are right, Rahul. I shouldn't stay tight-lipped. I would battle for my buddy Vedika. Once, she would get fine. I wouldn't spare those boys too. We all would file a complaint against those boys and protest for justice, so that the boys don't dare to do the same in future with any other girl. Priyanshi replied.

Yes Priyanshi! Now you are a grit girl. Let's ask for contribution. We would create posts at various social media sites and also seek for the help of news media. The News media published our posters and bank account number at various newspapers and sites. Many people would contribute to her life.

After a day, Ishaan informed to the Rahul over the call that,"We have received the collection of ten lakhs in a day. Despite that, we have to collect five lakhs more and only few hours left."

Everyone is worried and busy in finding out the ways to get five lakhs more.

Priyanshi asked, "what else we can do...?" We should figure out the ways quickly guys else it would be hard for us save Vedika's life.

"I am not getting any idea, Priyanshi." Rahul said.

Even me too ... Ishaan said.

I have got an idea. I will donate my blood to have money. I could do anything to shield my friend. Ananya said.

'Wow! That's a great idea, but you don't need to do that. I have some gold and diamond jewellery sets. I will be kept that on lease, and we would get around five lakhs from that.' Priyanshi replied.

"What, are you sure?" Rahul said.

Yes, damn sure. But, what will you speak to your parents?

I would tell everything to them. I know they would understand the circumstances and do not rebuff. They are so kind-hearted. Priyanshi reverted.

"Ok, great! Go ahead....!!" Ishaan said.

Priyanshi reached at home and explained everything to her parents. Her father reacted and said, but it's an exorbitant amount, my daughter.

So, what dad? Is it important than someone's life? And Vedika is very close to my soul. She is like my sister. I prefer not to lose her and I want to listen to her voice and want to look at her cute smile again. Please dad, I request you to help me out to shield her.

But beta ...!!!

Please dad, try to understand the situation. I would return all to you when I'll start earning money. But, help me out right now.

What if your daughter was at her place, and she was going through the same, and no one was there to help her out? Did you like that....???

Priyanshi beta... don't say these words. Whatever is mine is yours. You can draw off the jewellery from the locker and lease it out at nearest jewellery shop to protect your friend.

Thanks dad! I love you.

No thanks, my girl! Indeed, I am feeling proud to have you. You have such a great thought for your friend, and now leave, else you would reach late to the hospital.

Ok dad, I am going now.

I wish Vedika gets well soon. God bless her!

Priyanshi reached at hospital again.

All of them, have deposited money in a hospital. The Doctors began surgery in the night at 1o'clock.

Everyone there has not chewed even a bite of food from last two days. They are just crying, and pretending that, 'Vedika get well soon.'

The parents and the friends of Vedika are in trauma, thinking about the incident happened with Vedika.

Already two hours passed, but no one came out from operation theatre. The parents of Vedika just sit in agony and crying. The mother of Vedika has been ruptured from inside. It was hard for them to hide tears of themselves.

Priyanshi brings some juices and snacks from canteen so that everybody could have some foodstuff. She called everyone to have some snacks. But no one is ready to pick up even a single bite.

The entire night passed, and the doctors came out at 8a.m. around.

Everyone run towards surgeon hastily and asked, "Is Vedika fine now?" How was the surgery? Has it implemented successfully? Rahul asked.

Yes, it is, but right now, she is not in her senses. It would take at least 24 hrs to get into her senses. Doctor replied.

Ok, thanks, sir! Ananya and Rahul said.

Everyone seemed calm, but her parents were still outraged. They have forgotten their smile and just whimpering and sobbing. They seem to be shattered from inside. Nurses are bustled in looking upon Vedika, handing over her pills and other requirements.

Rahul gets coffee for everyone and proposed to have it. Everybody took a sip of coffee and felt rejuvenated.

But, the parents of Vedika still sounding worried and anxious.

Priyanshi offered them a packet of cookies along with a cup of coffee, and ask them to have it. They rebuffed to take it, but Priyanshi said, "I know you are worried, but at least have some food for your daughter. She is also feeling starving from inside. If you take food, her stomach would also get filled, so please have it."

Ok, we will take it beta. All of you are really sympathetic friends as you helped us a lot. Thanks to all of you, I hope you all stay like this and helped each other throughout the life. It was hard to get friends like you in this cruel and selfish world. So, I proud to have all of you along with us. Vedika is so lucky that she got friends like you.

"Thanks uncle! I know Vedika would get fine soon. So, just stop being lachrymose, wipe your face, and have some biscuits and coffee." Priyanshi said.

*****

CHAPTER TEN

Psychically Broken After a Catastrophe

After 24 hrs, The Surgeon went into the ICU room to have a look. "Is Vedika turn back into her senses?" The Doctors have extracted white cotton from her face to confirm if surgery had been taken place successfully.

After pulling out all the cotton from her face, the doctors determine that all the marks of acid attack weed out successfully. No marks could be conspicuous on Vedika's face now. But, she has received a distinct look which was entirely distinct from the previous one.

When Vedika had looked at her face in the mirror. She seemed shaky because she had squandered her ordinary view, and she didn't love this distinct look, but she didn't have any alternative except to hold her synthetic look. She was broken off profoundly.

Vedika urged to the doctor, "Could I hook up with my parents?"

Sure Vedika. Why not...? Dr. Sachin replied.

The Doctors had called her parents to meet her.

The parents of Vedika felt stunned when they had put up a glance over her face. They hadn't recognized Vedika at first glimpse, and sought to Doctors, "Is she Vedika, my daughter?"

"Yes, she is your daughter, Vedika." Dr. Sachin responded.

But, What had happened to her face? The Vedika's mother enquired.

"She had got a new look because of surgery. The natural face had been burnt badly, so it's hard to extract marks from that skin." Dr. Sachin responded.

The parents of Vedika appeared dismayed, but still didn't act so much as they could perceive that Vedika have been feeling dreadful. Instead of showing up them grieves, they said, "Wao! Vedika is just looking stunning with her new look." Haven't you felt the same Vedika?

Oh! Really, mom, did you like my current looks? I'm genuinely not feeling overjoyed with this look.

The mom said, "Oh! But why? My girl, you are truly looking so graceful." There is nothing to lament, and I am delighted that you are absolutely fine now. I had felt spooked when I received the news about this incident.

I know mamma, it's also not possible for me to bow out from this catastrophe ever. I couldn't forget those merciless individuals in my life.

The police had also arrived at the destination for inspection. They had enquired about everything, note down the points and draw up a document to file a FIR.

The friends of Vedika had reached to meet her. They kept silent and eyeballed Vedika for a few minutes. They don't know "what to say or what not?"

Rahul asked, "Are you ok, Vedika?"

Vedika replied. Yeah! Ok. But ...

What ok? Tell me Vedika. The Rahul asked.

I couldn't forget those ferocious folks. *'How did they transform my life within few minutes?'* And *'what about them?'* They had flown away from that place and living with no scary thought, till now.

Would they ever be captured......????

Would they be penalized for such an act...??? Would they also go through the same bitterness that I have experienced....???

Would I be able to look at them in the same plight when plunges of acid thrown on them, and they are drowning because of that....??? May be not yr....!! Vedika replied.

Everybody stands there, looking at her, felt dejected and couldn't stop tears from their eyes.

Simran turned ahead and gave a tight hug to Vedika. She added, "Don't feel weepy, Vedika. Everything would get fine. The culprits would be imprisoned for their deeds one day." Just wait and watch......!!!

I know, "They would never be punished, Simran." Vedika replied.

They would be penalized, Vedika. "All those vicious men would also go through the same torment in front of you. You would look at them drowning in front of you. It's my vow to you." Rahul replied.

Let see all that later. But, how are you all? Vedika asked.

Great yr...!; "I think you should take some food and juice now, and do rest for some time. It's not safe for you to communicate so much." Ishaan spoke.

Meanwhile, An Attendant turned inside and told, "You all need to step out so that I could give her medications, injection and meal to eat."

Ok, sure. Ma'am. Ishaan responded.

Ok, buddies! Let's walk out.

Bye Vedika. See you soon. Take care. Ishaan added.

Yeah! Bye friends. Vedika replied.

Vedika had consumed juice and porridge. Then, the nurse had given her medicines and injection for recovery.

The Doctor had informed to the parents of Vedika that, '*they could take her at home after a week.*' Till then, we will keep her under surveillance, and also given a prescription for Vedika.

Rahul picked up the prescription and went out with Ishaan to buy all the medicines.

Rahul said, "Yr Ishaan, what happened to Vedika?" I never thought that she would suffer a violent attack of acid. I have also become frightened from inside and thinking that, "What about those girls who suffer such attacks and don't even get treated because of such high charges in hospital?, What about the future of such girls?"

Maybe, it was impossible for them to get married because boys never get married to incinerated girl.

Indeed, they are maltreated in society. Ishaan replied.

The girls who didn't get treatment for such attacks, feels reluctant to live life and commit suicide too. In my point of view, these kinds of people who harassed girls physically, mentally and sexually should be encountered so that no one could take up such atrocities to innocent girls. Ishaan added.

*"You are correct. I hope everyone could think like you. Instead of scorning victim girls for such misdeeds, people should throw pebbles on such criminals."*Rahul replied.

They had come back to the hospital after purchasing the medications. They gave medicines to doctors. Then, they all went out to have a meal as they barely ingested anything from last few days.

The Mother of Vedika said, "Vedika's face burnt fiercely, and she had got some marks at her palm, neck and limbs too. Although, the face of Vedika has been recovered through surgery, but still she didn't get her natural look back. It could be clearly discernible that she went through surgery. I'm bothered by that, "Who will wed to her?"

Yeah! You are right,'Who would marry her?' The boy and his family always look for beautiful and a charming girl. 'Who would accept Vedika as daughter-in-law now?' The father of vedika said.

Rahul was taking notice of all this conversation by standing aside and couldn't stop his tears.

After a few minutes, he said, she would get someone definitely. Don't worry...!!!

No son, you don't have an idea, "How cruel this society is...?" Let me ask you, "Would you marry such a girl who had suffered acid attack and got burnt marks on her body?" Not only this, she had also been sexually assaulted.

Rahul gets silence at the moment and moves out after a while.

*****

CHAPTER ELEVEN

GRAPPLE WITH THE SOCIETY IS THOUGHT PROVOKING..!!!

Vedika reached to her home after a month. She had forgotten her smile.

People around her, were whispering about the incident what Vedika had suffered.

When Vedika listen dialogue among people that, Who would marry with her now...? The body of her had got so many marks of acid attack, and the face has been looking artificial.

The kids, when saw her, outrun from that place because they felt horrified. The neighbours reached at home and added, "Ohhh! What's this? She was looking monstrous."

One of the lady, Why don't you kill this girl? She has no life now.

Which of the College would admit her.....???
Which company would offer her a job....???

Who would accept her as a wife...???

Would she be able to give birth to children ever..??

And her terrified face could also become appalling and atrocious for anyone. Give her a tablet or an injection, so that she won't be able to awaken again.

When Vedika heard all this. She felt frightened. She enters the room and noticed herself in the mirror. She was looking so weird and bizarre. She burst into tears, and her heart broken into pieces. She squatted on the armchair, and cussing herself to be a girl in such a grotesque society.

On the next day, her friend, Rahul, came to his home to meet her.

Rahul said, "Hey, what's up?, How are you feeling now?"

She prefers to stay silent, and obscuring her face. She had neglected Rahul, and said, "Please Rahul, go from here. I don't want to talk to anyone."

But, what happen, Vedika? Are you not feeling ok? Rahul asked.

I said, "just go." Vedika reacted.

Okkk..,"I think, it's not the perfect time to communicate with you. I will come later, and took off from there." Rahul reacted.

Vedika again shattered into tears and felt depressed.

After a few weeks, Ananya and Simran had reached at her home. They had communicated with her, and console her to come out of this inferno, and start living your life in the same way you used to live before this incident.

I couldn't Ananya. If I would attend college, everyone would gawk at me, and further make fun of me. I am ok here. Please, leave me alone. I have not been in a condition to talk to anyone. Vedika replied.

So, how would you continue your study? What about your future? Simran asked.

I hadn't thought about that, but I will consider the same. Vedika replied.

The days go on, and a year passed. The psychic condition of Vedika kept on deteriorating. She hadn't fallen asleep for the last few nights. She didn't eat food. She had been feeling anxious and agitated.

She used to think that,"how would I suffer in this society? What would be my future, now?"

After a few days, Ishaan called her up, and asked Vedika, Are you ok?

Yes, I'm ok. Vedika replied.

So, when will you come back to college? Ishaan asked.

Never, I would never come back in the college. She replied.

But... why? Ishaan asked.

Because people would make fun of me. She replied.

Are you stupid? No one will do like this. Ishaan told.

Vedika cut the call and sit again, holding his head.

Ishaan, Ananya and Rahul reached at her home, and prompted her to come back to the college.

You should not think, "what the society would say ...!!" Rahul said.

It's your life. It's your career. If you wouldn't continue your study, your life would get hampered, not the life of society. You also have the choice to cover your face if you are feeling so weird. But don't sit at home. Ananya said.

Vedika seems to be convinced, and feeling calm after conversation.

On the next day, Ananya had arrived to pick her. Vedika grabbed her bag and covered her face with the scarf. When she walked out for a while, her scarf gets open and fall on the ground.

Everyone around her had stared at her. Some Children reacted like that she is a phantom, and some ladies are like, "Girls should not be sent to the college, they are born to sit at home and cook food. If you will send the girls at college, they would suffer such a monster act."

One lady noticed, "Is she is still going to the college after going through an incident?"

Hey girl...!! Are you not feeling ignominy while going to the college?

One old woman said, "You should sit at home and maintain dignity for the rest of the life. If something happened again, Who will take your responsibility?"

And some ladies just start whooping and gossiping that "Send your daughters out, and let them suffer acid attack, physical harassment, mental harassment, sexual harassment and eyes teaching. At this age, we got married, and become a mother of children, and also carry out household chores."

One old man interrupts, and said, "that's why I used to say that girls would be safe if they stay at home." The world beyond the boundaries of home is not safe at all for girls.

Another man interrupts, and stated, *"The role of girls is just to stay at home and gave birth to an offspring, cook meal, mob the floor and serve the needs of husband and in laws."*

One lady interrupt, and said, "I would not send my girl to the college ever, so that she doesn't suffer the same. I would find a bridegroom for her and carry out her engagement ceremony at the 14 -15 years of age.We should not send the girl at school and college too much, else they become pompous and cocky. She would also become domineering if they become educated and polished."

One lady said, *"Girls would remain as girl, they can't compare themselves with boys. If they move out from home and try to equate themselves with boys, they would suffer the same. That's why girls should sit at home."*

Rahul interrupt in between and said, "Would you hold your nonsense and folly talks with yourself?"

If you don't want to educate your girl child, make her sit at home and taught her to clean the utensils, wash the clothes, mob the floor and last but not the least, how to serve her husband and children.

But, keep your malarkey with yourself. We are sagacious and brainy enough to deal with a bad patch. We don't need your tip off.

Oho! Just see this boy. How ridiculous and arrogant this boy is?

Hey boy...! just listen. We have too much experience than you. We are elder than you. Don't you know how to respect elders and their views?

What's the benefits of your education if you can't respect your elders and their norms? Have you learnt all this from your parents? A man said.

Oh Really! Uncle, I think, you need to change your cast of minds. You should also need to learn, "how to respect girls...?" and support them, and take education by yourself first.

Then, you realize, "The Proper education means to respect a girl as much as you do it for boys. The education taught us to phase out and exterminate the non-scientific, illogical, and anecdotal norms of society."

Now, you, a dumb and idiot boy, would advise me, "what is right or wrong?" You are very young right now. You don't have any experience of the world till now. So, just be quiet, and accept what we are saying.

Uncle....! Just back off with your negative outlook.

Meanwhile, Vedika turns into a speechless and dumbstruck girl. She moves back towards her home. She had crumbled into pieces and starts screaming again. After a while, she closed the door, and going to cut the nerves of her hand.

But at the moment, Ananya reached there and stopped her. Then, she hugged Vedika tightly and said, "one day, you would get what you deserve. Don't even have a thought to commit suicide again."

After a few hours, when Vedika slept, Ananya moved out along with her friends and bought some books for Vedika.

Later, Ananya handed over the books to Vedika and said, "stay here, until you feel better, and continue your studies at home only."

You can also take the help of YouTube channel to grasp the concepts, and clear your doubts. But I hope you will get well soon, and come back to the college. Rahul added.

No, I will never come back. Thanks for everything that you guys had done for me, and take these books from here. I don't want to study and leave me alone.Vedika said.

So,"would you stay at home just because of these lewd and sordid minded people?","Would you spoil your career just because of outlaw and fallacious norms?"

When they declined to move out, Vedika pushed them away out of the room, and close the door. After that, she was squealing and shrieking.

Ananya, Ishaan, and Rahul couldn't stop their tears now. And after a few hours, they had left the home.

Suddenly, *Vedika got fainted, and fall on the ground.* Everyone around her enters the room, and wondering, "what happens to her ?"

They throw water on her face, and tried to bring her back into consciousness. They called the doctors immediately to diagnose her disease.

The doctor diagnosed her. He said, "it was just because of fragility and feebleness." She needs rest for some time. Don't put any kind of stress or pressure on her mind. Gave her juices and fruits daily to recover soon. The Doctor gave her prescriptions and told her to take a complete rest.

*****

CHAPTER TWELVE

TO BECOME VICTORIAN AFTER THE SMASH HIT

Vedika suffered depression for next three years. She had forgotten nothing. She went through surgery many times in the last few years. She never turned back towards her college life.

Meanwhile, Ishaan joined coaching institute for UPSC preparation. He was putting his day and night to qualify for the exam, but failed to accomplish his goals.

Ananya seeks the permission to start the business of clothing, but her parents refused, and asked her to gear up for government job exams.

Ananya was not so good at studies, so she didn't study by heart most of the time. Although, she tried her best, but couldn't qualify any government exams. She didn't understand the concept of social studies and maths. It was troublesome for her to memorize the concept of these two subjects. Apart from this, she prefers to do rote memorization of historical dates and other facts in the General Knowledge section. She tried for government exams consistently for two years, but result was nil. She hadn't shortlisted for any Government job.

She was turned into an irked and infuriated girl...!!!

She asked her father that she wants to drop out on the plan of government jobs, and want to start her own business. But, her parents again turned down the business idea, and responded, you are incompetent to qualify even a single entrance exam of government job, 'how would you get success in a business?'

Girls could only manage their homes, cook meal and wash clothes. They don't have calibre to deal with the responsibilities of business. I don't have any money to invest in your absurd idea. And, if you want to discontinue your preparation for government exams, then just get married, manage your home and serve to the needs of in-laws and husband.

When Ananya heard this, she was wondering, "What If I am a girl...?"

"Why Can't I manage business successfully...?"

"Do the boys born with some special features to handle the business..?"

"Is the success of any business depend on its gender?"

Many of the questions raised in her mind. But, she stayed silent, and move inside the room.

She has opened her laptop and looks for the history of successful businesswomen. When she fetches the information, and goes through it. She has realized, "it was the phenomenon that the parents were always a less supportive to the girl child." They hardly support their girl child to run the business. Furthermore,'*They are always ready to invest twenty to fifty lakhs in her marriage, but can't invest in her business.'*

The reason behind the less success rate of businesswomen are the myths and stereotypes prevail in our society.

The next day, she went out to take some food items and put a glance at the bank nearby.

She realized that, "What if I borrow the loan from the bank? They would surely provide the loan to me."

She moved inside the bank and fetches all the information and procedures to borrow the business loan. They asked her to carry a list of documents to have business loan.

On the next day, Ananya took the list of documents, and submitted for verification and further process.

Within a week, she received mail that her loan was approved. She was rapt, and started dancing on the floor. But, she concealed everything from her parents because she was petrified of their reaction.

After next 2 weeks, she had received the amount of business loan.

Then, she had moved to the registration office to carry out registration process to set up business. She had put all the formalities of registration into effect.

After completion of whole procedure of registration, she began her clothing business online.

She could not fetch good profits in initial years, but she had not lost the hope, till the end.

Later, she came up with the new designs in her clothing store along with additional offers to extend her business.

When the business reached at growth level, she put up additional products into her store like jewellery, bangles, makeup products, etc.

But one day, the father of Ananya gets to know about all this. And he enquired to Ananya, about everything. Ananya felt frightened, when her father enquired, about the business.

She had told all to her father, but as expected, the father rebuked her and told, *"Have I given you the birth to sell clothes?"*. "Don't you feel humiliated when you sell clothes after being an educated girl...?"

No papa, despite that, 'I have been feeling glad that I am a businesswoman and doing what I dreamt of.'

What's the sense of education in all this.......????

Does education say that a girl couldn't sell clothes......???

Oh! "Would you argue with me.....?"

I think you have grown up so much. We must look for a bridegroom for you, else you would work on something else that could harm our dignity. The father said.

Ananya realized, "she couldn't accomplish anything if she sticks around here. She puts the stuff in a bag and left the home to achieve her dreams."

One day, Vedika was scrolling the phone. She had looked at one video on YouTube, in which she saw that one girl who suffered acid attack turned into a successful businesswoman now, through which she gets an idea to achieve her dreams. She had started a YouTube channel through which she educates young children. She becomes the best educator in the entire country, after a few years, of consistent hard work.

And, "Ananya started living solely at a distant from her family. She hadn't taken food for some days, she didn't bed down for few days and she had also felt anguished for so many days."

But,"*within three and a half years, Ananya had created a wealth of 3 crore approx. She had also purchased a dream car and a well-accommodated house."* She had got engaged with Rahul, who become a successful Chartered Accountant.

But, Ishaan didn't qualify for UPSC exam, so he decided his luck for Bank exams. But after a few years of hard work, he didn't make it in bank exams too. The dreams of Ishaan never turned into reality. He felt frustrated, irked, and infuriated.

Later, he had become a schoolteacher because he left with no other preference. He always used to criticize and decry himself. He seemed to be agitated and disturbed because of so many breakdowns in life.

Apart from that, it was extremely painful for him to deal with the mental pressure of freakish comments put up by society because teaching was considered as a third-class job.

'Teaching job was considered as a suitable profession for girls as they can balance both home and job after marriage but not for boys...!!' He receives merely ten thousand as a salary at the end of a month.

On the other side, he had faced a lot of burden of expenses of marriage of his sister. In addition, he felt the pressure to serve the needs of his whole family. He had set up his own business, but failed to gain good profits. He had suffered a loss of 50 lakhs in a business in last 1 year, owing to which, he becomes bankrupt.

After 3 years, Ishaan had been suffering from so many diseases that he faced a heart attack in the midnight one day. He had left his splendid memories on the earth but fly away somewhere else.

*****

Author's Note

The novel is of imaginary character but fits to certain life facts that our teen is confronting now. The issues that our young generation face is:

First, they seldom get the help from kinsfolk to carry out their own daydreams. The parents have their own expectations and they placed the saddle of their notions on the scholar's perceiving.

The kinsfolk always turns into the dominant authoritarian of their offspring's life regardless of the factor "What their children wish to have in future? What their kids prefer to belong to, what their children thought of?". Ishaan lost his heart because he drops to fulfill the aspirations of his Father "of becoming IAS officer". This is the deep practice of India that, "whatever the kinsfolk expects from their offspring, the juvenile desire to fulfill that and neglect about his own preference, desires and inclinations which generate a perverse relation between the kinsfolk and the adolescents."

Second, the prospect of adolescent is expected based on gender somewhere like "If Ananya wants to become Businesswomen, everyone prognosticate she can't manage it because she is a girl".

So, what if she is a girl? Girls have the same potentials what boys have. Girls are corresponding to son. She can work out everything that a boy can work.

Third, girls are most often considered wrong regardless of the factors "whether she had made something reprehensible." Vedika encountered an incident and afterward she too suffered criticism from the community for moving out while she wouldn't have carried amiss. The individuals are condemning her for reaching out for classes.

But why ...?

"Had she made anything wrong...?"

"Had she flung the caustic attack?"

If she made nothing illegal. Then why should she lay at home and felt ashamed? Why can't she be viewed the same as before.

In my point of view, those street Romeos should be driven to lie at home so that they couldn't harm any other girl. But they all have set free because they are lads. In crisp, our community never put guilt on boys owing to which disputes are multiplying at crest level. They criticize always girls for non-maintaining social norms if they encounter any type of molestation.

Last, but not the least that a boy and a girl can also be the great allies. Our society refuses that a boy and a girl can't be perfect companions. They are considered as love birds if they hang together, but indeed it is not. True friendship still prevails between a boy and a girl in our community.

The purpose of the novel is to reveal the realism of community rules that "How are the youngsters getting depressed because of norms?"

The pre-accepted sentiments of society drag the teen into blazes of fire, but yet it continues to exist. The kinsfolk should admit the facts that the world is evolving and they should let the youngster free to build up and get succeed on their own wish.

I have come across such circumstances many times in life. So, I figured out to share the issue in the book one day. *I hope it would contribute to a revolution in the world of many juveniles. And development in the way of life of one individual can contribute to the transformation to the entire world.*

AUTHOR'S NOTE

*****

Ingram Content Group UK Ltd.
Milton Keynes UK
UKHW010740180523
421954UK00001B/7

9 798887 725291